BARRACK TWO

ELYSE HOFFMAN

ISBN 978-1-952742-03-3 (ebook)

Project 613 Publishing
Project613Publishing.com

PROJECT613

Dedicated to my mother and father for their enduring support
To my grandfather whose stories I never heard
To all of the women who suffered during the Holocaust
And to God, Who makes all stories

BARRACK TWO

"I'm pregnant."

The announcement struck Vilém Rehor like a sledgehammer to the gut. He stood before his girlfriend, who cradled her not-yet-showing belly and pronounced her pregnancy with restrained fear. He had treated her well tonight: dinner, a walk in the park, and now they stood by a water fountain, Jana grimacing, Vilém gawking at her.

He gave her a moment to declare that she was just kidding. When she didn't, he clenched his jaw. A whirlwind of emotions went through him. Happiness, love, nervousness, excitement...it all hit at once and he was shocked when his body still managed to move.

"Well...I guess this is appropriate, then," he said. He reached into his pocket and pulled out a small box, dropping to one knee. The atmosphere changed immediately: Jana lit up like a star and Vilém grinned.

"Oh, you asshole!" Jana screamed. She heard laughter nearby and looked towards the bushes. Erik,

Vilém's best friend, was hiding in the thicket, recording the proposal on his phone.

"Now, I warn you: I'm too broke to buy a ring, so…" Vilém opened the box, revealing a sapphire flower, pressed and preserved in a little glass oval. Jana realized what it was right away: Klammer's flower, the one he had given Vilém's great-grandfather.

"How…?" she whispered.

"Good question! I think Rebecca had it. I looked through the attic at Mom's house and recognized the tin," Vilém said. Jana looked at the box again and realized it wasn't a box, but an almost century-old tin. She could barely make out a duo of cherries printed on the front. An ancient cough-drop tin. Sam had saved it, stored the precious flower in it, and now Vilém was offering it to his beloved.

"Vilém, I can't take this!"

"You can if you become my wife!" Vilém said. "By the way, wanna be my wife?"

"Yes, I wanna be your wife, dummy! I love you!" she cried, lunging at him. The now-engaged couple toppled to the sidewalk.

"Congrats, buddy!" Erik laughed. "Jana, be careful, don't kill him before the wedding!"

"I'll try!" giggled Jana, rolling off her fiancée. She grabbed his hand and kissed his knuckles, and Vilém had never felt so happy.

Jana hugged the cough-drop tin and the preserved cornflower close to her heart, tears falling from her eyes. She squealed as though she had just won the lottery.

"Oh, I'm gonna be a wife!" she cried, grasping her

fiancé's hand and pressing it to her belly. "I'm gonna be a wife and you're gonna be a daddy!"

And then there was that. That...well, *that* he hadn't been expecting, but Vilém wasn't disappointed. Not in the least. His old life as an immature young adult was over, and now...now he was going to have a little bundle of responsibilities.

"I'm *so* not ready!" he laughed as he pulled his wife-to-be into a hug. "I'm so not ready, this is gonna be crazy! I'm gonna be a dad!"

He stood up with a hoot, announcing to the smiling onlookers and everyone else in earshot, "I'm gonna be a dad!"

"So lemme guess: 'I forgot a condom just one time.'"

"Oh, shut up, Erik."

"Am I wrong? C'mon, man, I know ya'."

"...Twice."

"Lucky you! Ha!" Erik smacked his friend on the shoulder. Jana had gone back to the sweet shop to tell her grandmother that she was engaged. Erik, meanwhile, had dragged Vilém to the bar to celebrate the merry occasion.

"Happy accident!" Vilém said, taking a swig of beer. "Jesus Christ, I'm like...happy and I feel like I'm back in school about to take a pop quiz! It's a totally alien feeling, I can't even really describe it. I'm gonna be married and a dad! Wow..."

He grinned at his friend and said, "I'm an adult now!"

Erik snickered, clinking his mug against Vilém's. "Always knew you'd mature before me. I'm gonna be best man, right? And godfather?"

"Jana's probably gonna wanna raise the little one Jewish, Erik, and I'm deferring to her."

"Damn it!"

"Look, considering where I work, if I can bring a brand-new little Jew into the world, I'll feel a little better."

"Ha! Every new baby Jew makes Hitler spin in his grave. Oh, speaking of your job, though: I didn't wanna bring this up since you're celebrating, but I got some info that may help you complete your mission."

Vilém shoved his mug away and forced his jubilant spirit to settle. For months, he had been struggling to fulfill Joseph Klammer's last wish and give Doctor Yosef the recognition he deserved. Unfortunately, Vilém still didn't know the Doctor's full name, and even combing through the Camp's archives had yielded nothing. Kommandant Gerber had covered his tracks well. There was nothing about Raya, Iveta, Little Martin, or the Doctor-Rabbi. The Nazi Regime's power to destroy so much information, to annihilate lives physically and in writing, was almost as impressive as it was frightening. It was a small miracle that historians knew as much about the Holocaust as they did given the lengths the SS had gone to covering it up.

"So," Erik said, pulling out a small piece of paper. "I get a call to fix a toilet at the hotel. I go in and the room's guest is this old guy, like really old, older than

Granny Illa. German guy, but y'know, there are Germans who live here, not a big red flag. We end up chatting and I ask him why he's in town. He says he comes once a year to leave flowers for Sergeant Klammer, says the guy saved his life. Not a big deal, y'know, must be one of the Jews from the Freedom Train, but he ends up leaving a tip for me with his credit card and look…"

Erik pulled out the receipt and pushed it towards Vilém. The name of the customer was printed in bold at the bottom of the paper: Helmut Schwartz.

"You're kidding…" whispered Vilém. Schwartz, the young Nazi that Joseph had gone back for, the foolish child who had been unquestioningly loyal to the Nazis.

"I mean, I know Schwartz isn't an uncommon name, but it's a little…much," said Erik.

"If it *is* him, he's taking a risk coming here every year," Vilém observed, scowling at the former Nazi's name. "He may have been young back then, but he's still a war criminal. He must have a warrant on his head."

"He must…but he's old. Maybe at this point he doesn't care if he dies in a cell."

"Well," said Vilém, leaning back and smirking as he curled the receipt around his finger. "It would be a shame if someone *happened* to turn him in. Unless he has some good info or could give a statement."

"Vil, you're becoming a history vigilante. I love it. Let's get to the hotel before he drops dead."

"Hey, Herr Schwartz, can I come back in? I'm the plumber from earlier."

Vilém scowled as the old man opened the door to his suite and invited Erik and his "associate" inside. SS Private Helmut Schwartz had not aged gracefully: liver spots covered his bald head, his Aryan blue eyes had weakened to the point where he needed inch-thick glasses to see, and he had developed a Quasimodo-like hunch. He smiled at the two Czechs with such sweetness that nobody would have suspected he once considered their race undesirable.

"Oh, I'm sorry, I've tried not to use it," Schwartz said, scooting towards the restroom, but stopping halfway and taking a seat on the foot of his bed. "This happens every time I come here, something breaks, but it *is* the only hotel in town so...can't be picky."

"I imagine you've experienced worse in your life-time," Vilém said. "Private Schwartz."

It was a miracle the old Nazi didn't keel over of a heart attack right then. He froze, his weary eyes flitting from Vilém to Erik.

Erik retreated into the bathroom to let Vilém do his work. Vilém leaned against the door, blocking off the Nazi's only escape.

"Am...I under arrest?" Schwartz asked.

"You should be," Vilém snarled. "You should have been arrested decades ago."

"Yes...you're right," sighed Schwartz, looking down at his gnarled hands. "I should have. If I were a good man, I would have turned myself in after I realized what I was, but...I only have one life, and I didn't feel like spending it in prison."

"Those Jews only had one life too," Vilém accused, pointing in the direction of the Camp. "You and your comrades took that from them. And here you are...old. Must be nice. Do your kids know?"

"I have none."

"Good," scoffed Vilém, pleased that Schwartz never had and never would feel the explosion of uncertain joy that came with becoming a father. "So you're here for Klammer?"

"I can explain..."

"You don't have to," Vilém said. "I know you were on Klammer's Train, and I know he shot you, then saved you. I know he took you back to the Camp and you sold him out. I know it's *your* fault he's dead."

What little color still clung to the old man's face faded. "H-how could you possibly know that?"

"I know a lot," Vilém said with a dismissive wave of his wrist.

"But the Kommandant told everyone *I* captured Klammer! N-nobody knows what really happened except for me!"

"That so?" Vilém said. "I don't suppose there are more tidbits of history that *only you* know..."

Schwartz folded his hands on his lap, trembling. "So am I under arrest? Is this an interrogation?"

"In a way. You come here every year to honor Klammer, so I assume you've had something of a change of heart."

"Of course!" exclaimed Schwartz. "Listen, I know I'm a terrible person. I've tried my best all my life to make up for what I did as a boy. I've worked, I've given to charity, I've given my time and my blood...I've tried,

7

and I think I've done better outside of jail than I would have inside. I know I can't make up for what I did to Sergeant Klammer and those people during the war..."

"*People*," Vilém repeated, rolling the word on his tongue and nodding slowly. "All right, I guess you *have* changed. And you're right: there's nothing you can do to make up for it, but I'm not going to have you arrested. That's not my job, and I don't know you well enough to decide how much you've really repented. All I know is you're here, and you owe Klammer. So do I, and I'm trying to help him settle an old wish."

"Wish...?"

"Long story short: Klammer had help organizing the capture of the Auschwitz Train, a man named Doctor Yosef who used to work for the Kommandant's...'son.'"

"Little Martin?"

"That's the one. The Doctor distracted the Nazis while Klammer shot you assholes in the back."

"Oh...he was the man who jumped..." Schwartz whispered.

"Precisely, and Klammer wanted to make sure he went down as a hero."

"How do you know that? Did Klammer keep a diary or something? He didn't speak much after we got back to the Camp, and his mother..."

"My great-grandpa Sam was his closest friend," Vilém explained, not precisely lying, but also avoiding the topic of ghosts all together. He didn't have time to explain the afterlife to the old Nazi.

"Oh...I see..." Schwartz mumbled. "Well, I *do* know who you're talking about. What do you need to know?"

"His full name, firstly."

"Oh! Right! I forgot Little Martin just called him 'Doctor Rabbi.' It was Yosef Doubek, he was from a little Jewish village in the south."

"*What?*"

Erik voiced Vilém's thoughts perfectly as he burst out of the bathroom, his eyes bulging.

"*Doubek?*" he cried, gawking at Vilém. "Like your crazy boss Doubek? *That* Doubek?!"

"Doubek's a common enough last name, it may be a coincidence," Vilém muttered, trying to maintain a calm facade even as shock almost made his jaw drop. "Did the Rabbi have a daughter?"

"He did, yes. We weren't allowed to touch her, that was the deal he had with Kommandant Gerber. I think her name was Alica."

"Yep...that's Ms. Doubek's first name," sighed Vilém, running a hand through his messy dark hair. "That doesn't make any sense...if his daughter's the museum's director, why was it so impossible to find anything about him?"

"If it were *my* dad, I would'a made an exhibit just for him," said Erik. Vilém chewed on his thumbnail, pondering this revelation. Ms. Doubek might have been a bitch, but if she really was the Rabbi's daughter, she could be helpful. She could offer trustworthy testimony about what her father had done, and then it would be easy to fulfill Klammer's wish.

"Listen," Vilém said, gesturing for Erik to take out his phone and start recording. "We're not going to have you arrested, but Joseph Klammer wanted the world to know the truth. I need you to give me your testimony. Can you do that? For him?"

9

Schwartz clutched the bedspread with trembling hands, shaking his head. But he looked out the window, towards the Camp, and Vilém could see guilt chew at the ex-Nazi's soul until he had no choice but to consent.

"For him, of course. I'll tell you anything you want to know."

"Good," said Vilém, grabbing a chair from a nearby desk and sitting across from the former SS officer. "First question: do you know who 'David' is?"

Private Schwartz did not know who 'David' was. In fact, he could hardly be called a well of knowledge. As a mere Private, he had not been privy to most of the Kommandant's grand secrets, but he was able to testify that Doctor Doubek had existed, that he had worked for Sergeant Klammer, and that he had helped save those four hundred people on the Auschwitz Train.

With a copy of the footage in hand, Vilém went to work. He weaved through the crowds of students, mourners, and amateur historians.

"Hey!" he shouted at the day guard. "You know where Doubek is?"

"The Kommandant?" snickered the day guard. "Barrack Two, women's exhibit."

"Thanks," sighed Vilém, rolling his eyes at the nickname. Though Ms. Doubek had certainly earned the derision of her employees, after everything he had experienced and after getting to know just how evil the real

Kommandant had been, that epithet made Vilém's gut churn.

He trudged into Barrack Two, which was a barrack he tended to avoid. The barrack, which had once housed over a hundred women, now featured an exhibit on women's experiences during the Holocaust. As mothers, as daughters, as survivors.

Vilém shivered and averted his eyes from one placard that offered an article about sexual assault in the Camp. Since the prisoners had by and large been "dirty Jews", it had been rare, but not unheard of, for the guards to take advantage of the denizens of Barrack Two. Several SS officers had been arrested for offenses against female prisoners. Not because they committed rape, of course, but because they betrayed their pure German blood, forcing themselves on undesirables. To the Nazi Regime, raping a Jew was equivalent to bestiality.

Vilém inhaled sharply and forced himself to look at the pictures of the shaved, skinny women. Fire rose up in his chest when he saw images of little girls being pulled from their mothers' arms. He looked at the formerly faceless women and saw Jana. He looked at the sobbing little girls and a paternal flare consumed his heart as he imagined his potential daughter amongst them.

He bit his bottom lip, looking into the women's eyes, trying to find a young Ms. Doubek.

"Rehor! What are you staring at?"

Vilém whirled around. Ms. Doubek had snuck up behind him. She looked as angry with life as ever, but for once Vilém didn't scoff at her attitude. If she was the very same Alica Doubek who had lived in this horrid barrack during the Holocaust, he was impressed. If he had lived through what she had, he wouldn't have been able to work at the Camp.

"Hello, Ms. Doubek," he said. The old woman raised an unkept eyebrow and snorted.

"Don't try to soften me up, I know what happened," huffed his boss. "Ms. Sladký called me earlier and bitched my ear off, told me to be nice to you because you're going to be her grandson-in-law soon, and you're apparently giving her a great-grandchild."

She jabbed at him with a pencil. "I always figured you were the irresponsible sort. I hope you don't expect me to give you time off for a wedding *and* paternity leave. I'm not going to pay for your bad decisions."

"'Bad decisions'?" repeated Vilém with a smirk, more amused than offended. Doubek snarled and pressed her pencil into his chest so forcefully he could feel the lead stabbing into his skin.

"Bad! Decisions!" she snapped, emphasizing each word with a stab. "And you'd better not even think of dragging little Dumbass Junior to the Camp and have him or her or it pitch a fit and ruin the atmosphere!"

"I'm not gonna bring my *baby* to a concentration camp, ma'am...who does that?"

"Irresponsible morons who have children before they can afford a babysitter, that's who!" Doubek declared, tapping her pencil against his chest one last time before tucking it back into her suit pocket. "I see them every day. One of these days, I'm gonna give you the day shift, Rehor. Then you can see the shit I have to put up with from the general public."

"I'm sure I have it easy at night, ma'am," chuckled Vilém.

"Was that sarcasm?"

"Honestly, no, I don't think you're wrong," Vilém said. "But Ms. Doubek, my personal life's really not important."

"Precisely: that's why I'm warning you not to bother me about it. Also, please tell your fiancée's grandma to stop calling the Camp! I know her sister died here, but that doesn't give her the right to tell me how to do my job!"

"Uhm...sure, ma'am. I'll get on that. But actually, I wanted to talk to you about *your* family. You see," Vilém pulled the flash drive out of his pocket and offered it to the director. "I've been doing a bit of independent research and collecting some testimonies, and I found some info about a man that I think is your father, Rabbi-Doctor Yosef Doubek. He helped Sergeant Klammer save the Jews on..."

Before he could say another word, Ms. Doubek grabbed the drive and threw it to the floor. Vilém yelped in shock as she brought her boot down on the drive, shattering it with a single stomp.

"What the Hell?!" cried Vilém, and a few visitors gawked at the altercation, some pulling their phones out of their pockets and snagging a video.

"*Come here*," Ms. Doubek snarled, grabbing her employee by the arm and dragging him out of Barrack Two. She pulled him behind the wooden structure and shoved him against the outer wall.

"Listen," she growled, shoving her finger in his face. "And listen well: my father lived as a fool, he died as a fool, and he deserves to be remembered as a fool. I've done him a favor by making sure he's forgotten. I've put up with your weird shit too long, boy. If you start digging into my life, I will fire you, and I will make sure you and your new little family starve. Understood?"

Vilém might have been intimidated a year ago, but experiencing the lives of Holocaust victims had hardened him to such relatively meager threats. He squinted down at his boss. Behind the anger, behind the seething, behind the clenched teeth, there was something else: sadness.

Of course, probing would do no good. Better to wait. Wait and hope that someone long gone would offer him answers tonight.

"Understood, ma'am. I'm sorry."

"Good," she huffed, straightening up and combing her fingers through her gray hair. "Now enough playing amateur historian. Get your flashlight and get ready for work! And if I even suspect that you've gone anywhere near my office..."

"I'll stick to the barracks, ma'am. Don't worry."

Ms. Doubek grunted. Her dark eyes darted to Barrack Two and Vilém saw a slight shiver wrack her body before she turned and stomped over to a group of day guards, screeching at them for lollygagging.

Vilém waited behind the barrack to make sure Ms. Doubek was busy harassing the other employees before he snuck back into Barrack Two. Since the ghosts typically showed up in a barrack that held some significance to them, he assumed Barrack Two would yield something.

"C'mon, Doctor," he whispered as the sun set and

14

the Camp became empty once more. "Give me something here...."

Once the gates were locked, the lights were off, and Vilém was seemingly left alone, he started wandering around Barrack Two with his eyes closed, touching every corner, every artifact, every picture.

Right when he was about to give up, his hands found a cluster of pictures displayed near the back of the barrack. He sensed something, though just barely. While the other spirits had been eager to chat, this one seemed intent on making himself scarce. Vilém smiled and sunk to his knees, getting comfortable before calling out.

"Doctor Doubek?"

He heard the spirit unleash a sigh so heavy he might have been holding it since the war.

I guess it's my turn.

"So do you ghosts talk to each other...?"

Never, but I knew Joseph was still here. I never talked to him, though. I tried, but I couldn't. It seems you have a gift.

"Somehow," sighed Vilém. "I guess Ilona spoke to Iveta, but I can talk to ghosts I don't have any connection to. It's...weird, but I hope I'm putting this 'gift' to good use. Speaking of good...y'know, it's kinda funny, you and Klammer. Joseph and Yosef. The same name, but very different people. And yet...you're both heroes."

A chill struck Vilém's heart, and he could practically feel the ghost shake its ethereal head.

I'm no hero. I'm many things, but I'm no hero.

"Don't tell me I'm gonna have to give you the same speech I gave Klammer."

Oh, boychik, you have no idea what I did. Joseph's sins were all committed with the best of intentions. He always did what he thought was noble. Me? No. There's a reason my daughter despises me.

"Enlighten me, please, Rabbi," Vilém begged.

I'm...not sure you'd understand. And...I don't want to be judged.

"Sir, whatever you did, you did it during the Holocaust. I can't promise I won't judge you, but I'll take the circumstances into account."

Are you a father, young man?

Vilém smiled, that now almost-familiar feeling of uncertain joy filling his soul. "I will be very soon."

Mazel tov! Well, then maybe you will understand. Very well, but please do not become as angry as my little Alica.

"I can promise that, I don't think that'd be physically possible," Vilém vowed. The

Rabbi's ghost chuckled softly.

Very well...hm...I think this all began when Alica was born.

Vilém felt as though he had been gently pushed. He fell and fell until finally, he found himself sitting in a dimly-lit synagogue sanctuary.

He was seeing the world through the Rabbi's eyes, feeling what he had felt a lifetime ago, and the intense clash of emotions that the Rabbi was experiencing was dizzying. Pain beyond measure...and love so overwhelming he felt like his chest might implode. The Rabbi was sitting on a small staircase that led to a clear glass arc, holding a little bundle in his arms.

He pulled back a bit of the blanket, revealing a baby's face. Ms. Alica Doubek. Only a few hours old.

It was a wonderful day...and a terrible day. My little Alica came at the cost of her mother.

"Oh...I'm sorry." Vilém shivered at the notion,

mentally thanking God for letting him live in an era where death during childbirth was so rare. He couldn't imagine what he would do without Jana, with the baby...he was already certain he was going to fuck up being a father, being a single father would destroy him.

It was more than a lifetime ago, boychik. I've come to terms with it. But it meant that Alica was to be my only child, all I had left in the world.

The Rabbi leaned down and kissed his newborn baby's forehead. "I'll always protect you, Alica, my little sunshine."

Vilém might have laughed under different circumstances. "Little sunshine?"

I always called her that, and when she was little, she was. Even without her mother, Alica was a little ray of light. In the community, I was known for being somewhat liberal. I was a man of science and God, a doctor and a Rabbi. I believed that knowledge should flow freely, to boys and girls alike, and while many Rabbis reserved their classrooms for boys only, I taught any child who wanted to learn about our faith. My little Alica was my best student.

"Children!" A new memory started. Rabbi Doubek was clapping his hands together, sending chalk dust flying into his face. He let out an exaggerated cough, causing the children that sat before him to giggle. Boys in kippahs, sporting sidelocks, sat beside little girls wearing head coverings. They all held notebooks and pencils. Rabbi Doubek's eyes fell upon a little girl in the front row, a little girl with curly brown hair, chocolate-colored eyes, and a smile that made the Rabbi's heart melt.

"Aww...she was cute," Vilém confessed as the Rabbi tenderly gazed at seven-year-old Alica Doubek.

The Rabbi turned to look at an illustration he had made on the blackboard. A picture of a woman standing atop a wall, throwing a goofily-drawn severed head down to a waiting soldier. The head had X's for eyes and a tongue sticking out the side of his mouth, somewhat alleviating the morbidity of the drawing.

"Now!" the Rabbi said. "For today's lesson, we are going to discuss the permissibility of..."

"Cutting someone's head off?" one little boy inter-rupted. A wave of giggles went through the little class-room and the Rabbi shook his head.

"Close, but no, Chassed. Today we will discuss the incident of Sheva Ben Bichri and what his story teaches us about sacrifices. Now, since I assume you all read your Tanakh passage for class today..."

The Rabbi shot an accusatory glare towards one particular nose-picker, who blushed and hid his face behind his Bible.

With a chuckle, the Rabbi continued. "I'll keep it short: Sheva Ben Bichri rebelled against King David, and when David's forces tried to capture him, he hid in the city of Abel. This is where we learn the story of the Wise Woman of Abel. When King David's forces started to sack the city, threatening to destroy it, she took it upon herself to make a deal with David's commander to save the city and all within. She convinced the people of Abel to behead Sheva Ben Bichri, and they tossed his head over the wall. Thus, Abel was saved."

The Rabbi pointed with a ruler towards the picture he had drawn. "Now, what we must ask ourselves is:

was this a mitzvah or a sin? Are we permitted to give up one for the lives of many? The Talmud teaches us that should someone say to us, 'Go kill so-and-so or I will kill you', we are not permitted to do so. One man's blood is just as red as another's, and it is not permissible for us, as humans, to say that we are more worthy of life than another human. Only God, in all of His wisdom, may decide that."

"Papa...err, Rabbi!" Alica chirped, shoving her hand into the air. The Rabbi beamed at his daughter's enthusiasm and gestured for her to speak.

"So, Papa, the Talmud says we have to *shev ve'al ta'aseh* — sit and do nothing — if that happens. If a gentile comes and says, 'Give us two Jews', we're not allowed to do that even if they threaten all the Jews. So...we all just have to sit and do nothing and let more people die?"

"In a way, Alica."

"Well, I'm confused, then: why didn't God punish the city of Abel for killing the rebel?"

"A very good question, Alica, and you're right. The Talmud teaches us that we must not cast lots to choose who lives and who dies. Now, Abel's situation is different. We learn from Maimonides in the *Code of Jewish Law* that if, say, a group of Jews is traveling and come across a group of gentiles, and the gentiles say, 'Give us one of you, or you will all die', then all must die, for we, as men and Jews, cannot decide whose life is worth more."

"But," he continued, "if they come upon the Jews and say, 'Give So-And-So or we will kill you all', then it is permissible to give that specified person over, for then we are not deciding who is more worthy of life, but we are like the Wise Woman of Abel. And if we are the one

19

singled out in such a situation, we are obliged to die for the community, for the greater number of Jews. But it is never permissible to kill for numbers."

The pupils nodded and scribbled down the teaching. Alica finished her notes fastest, smiling up at her father once she was done. She looked at him like he was Moses, like he was the greatest man who had ever lived.

I know she's a very different woman now, but when she was a girl, Alica was happy. She loved school, loved life...loved me. She adored me. I really was her hero.

A dust cloud of chalk whisked the memory away, and a new one took its place. Doctor Doubek was kneeling before a young boy, tending to the child's broken arm while his mother hovered nearby.

"Papa!" Alica's voice cut through the Doctor's focus. He turned and saw that his daughter was standing in the doorway, sporting a black eye.

"Alica, who did that?" he cried, and Vilém almost tumbled out of the memory. The fear and anger that the father felt upon seeing his child hurt was so intense it was almost painful.

The Doctor barely heard the injured boy's mother snap at him. He ignored her harsh plea and abandoned his patient, kneeling before his daughter and cupping her face in his hands. Alica laughed.

"Papa, I just fell off my bike!" the girl cried, pointing to the little boy. "David needs your help!"

Vilém's heart somersaulted at the name, but he reminded himself that he was looking into the memories of a Rabbi from a Jewish village. There were probably a dozen Davids that had nothing to do with Klammer. Broken-Armed David's face was slightly foggy. The

Rabbi's attention had been so focused on Alica that everything else seemed cloudy by comparison.

"R-right..." muttered the Rabbi, and he turned his attention back to David, listening with a hammering heart as his wounded daughter skipped away, humming happily.

Nothing seemed to trouble Alica. She was always singing, always bouncing, always dancing...oh, she had two left feet, but she danced like she was possessed and it was so lovely to watch. She loved American music even though she couldn't understand a word of it. This one song, sung by Billy Cotton, it went, "Smile darn ya smile!" It was her favorite, she loved it! Every time it came on the radio...

"Oh, Papa, it's the song!"

A new memory formed from the darkness: the Rabbi was resting in what must have been his study, reading a Hebrew book and sitting in a cozy chair beside a crackling radio. A bouncy American tune filled the whole house and Alica bolted into the study, pushing his book aside.

"Oh, sunshine, you'll make me lose my spot!" the Rabbi complained, though he couldn't repress a small smile as she grabbed his hands and pulled him to his feet.

"Dance, Papa, c'mon!" she laughed as Cotton's voice urged her on.

"Smile darn ya smile!
Y'know this great world is a good world after all!"

Vilém could hardly believe his eyes as he watched little Ms. Doubek move like she was made of water, swaying and spinning and kicking her legs into the air. The Rabbi tried his best to keep up with her enthusiastic movements, but he was no match for his little sunshine.

"C'mere, you crazy girl!" he cried, grabbing her waist and lifting her into the air, spinning her around and around.

"Papaaa, I'm dizzy!" she squealed. He set her back on the ground and she grabbed his hand once more, twirling around and kicking her leg up.

> *"Things are never black as they are painted*
> *Time for you and joy to get acquainted...*
> *So make life worthwhile,*
> *Come on and smile, darn ya—KKKHHHHHHHHHT!"*

But just as Alica was finishing her dance with another kick, she spun too close to the radio and ended up kicking the machine right off the tabletop. It fell to the ground, and the jazzy beat became terrible static.

"Oh, Alica!" sighed the Rabbi. "Look what you did, you crazy girl!"

"Whoops..." muttered Alica sheepishly, and even though she had destroyed what must have been the 1930s equivalent of a giant television, she refused to stop following the song's directive. She still smiled.

We were very happy...at least at first. We lived amongst our own. No gentiles in town, and when gentiles did come to visit, they were always sent right to me. I had spent my youth in Prague, learning medicine, learning about the gentile world. I learned Czech and German, and I learned how to please the gentiles.

"Errr...sorry," Vilém squeaked, suddenly weighed down by gentile guilt.

You're not Jewish?

"One-fourth, my grandfather was a Jew. I'm gonna marry a Jew and my kid's gonna be a Jew...but, uhm, I don't really believe in anything."

I don't blame you one bit.

A new memory appeared. The Rabbi sat across from a blonde couple, obvious gentiles, in the midst of what must have been his kitchen. His eyes flitted to the nearby living room, where Alica was playing with the gentiles' daughter.

In contrast to the Rabbi's study, his entertaining area was a synagogue of science: every bookshelf boasted medical tomes, every painting featured plants and animals, and statues of eminent doctors and scientists decorated the tabletops. A silver Newton's Cradle sat on a coffee table in the living room. The Rabbi had been very careful not to let his Jewishness show in the spaces where gentile guests were wont to trod, instead opting to make himself look as cultured and Western as possible.

"Doctor...or, Rabbi," the gentile man said. The Rabbi chuckled.

"Yosef will do, Herr Muller!"

"Yosef," Herr Muller said, gesturing to the scientific finery around the room. "I have to say, I never thought that a Jew in such a...primitive community could be so civilized."

"Oh, Herr Muller, I promise I'm not the only one," the Rabbi said. "I know from my travels that even in the great cities, not everyone is privileged with adequate schooling. Such is the case with many Jews. But my people, we are known for our curiosity. We thirst for knowledge even when it seems to contradict our faith."

"You may be better than the Catholics, then," chuckled the German woman. "Thank you for inviting us into your home, I feel like we've learned a lot. Oh, it makes all the silliness going on in the Fatherland seem so much worse, though."

"Silliness?" the Rabbi queried.

"Oh, you haven't heard?" Herr Muller said with surprise.

"I'm afraid news travels slowly, and my radio has been on the fritz for weeks thanks to my lovely daughter!" Doctor Doubek gestured towards Alica, smiling fondly. Little Ms. Doubek blushed and giggled.

"It was an accident!" she squeaked, and Herr Muller snickered.

"Oh, how many times have I heard *that* one?" he cried, winking at his daughter. "In all seriousness: our leader, the Führer, he won't be satisfied until we take back everything that was stolen from us."

"'Stolen'?" the Rabbi repeated, his voice an octave too high pitched. Herr Muller took a slow, thoughtful sip from his wine glass.

"Well, I agree with the Führer where that is concerned," he said. "These lands belonged to us Germans, we ruled them well and justly...and I think it's our right to rule them again."

"Oh, love, please!" Muller's wife groaned. "I was having fun, a fun cultural exchange without politics..."

"Politics *is* culture, my dear," Muller said, and the Rabbi nodded.

"Truth be told, Herr Muller, our village has been

here so long, under so many different figureheads," Doctor Doubek said. "If this Hitler fellow is a decent leader and he wants to rule over us, we likely won't notice or mind."

"Unfortunately, the Führer, for all of his brilliance, has let silly race-baiting cloud his judgment," Herr Muller explained. "He cares about the German people, but instead of focusing on the French and the Brits, he's honed in on the Jews. We came here because we wanted to see if he was correct about your people, and happily I've found that he's mistaken...but..."

The German clenched his jaw and glanced at the cheerful, ignorant children. He beckoned for the Rabbi to lean close. When he did, Muller whispered, "I fear that your people would not do well if we took over. And I know we will...so please, be careful."

"Listen," Muller continued after a moment of contemplation. "If you or your daughter need help, drop my name. Dietrich Muller, brother of SS Lieutenant Alois Muller. My brother isn't nearly as intellectually curious as me, believes everything he's told, but he loves me and respects me...and he still owes me for breaking my wrist when we were children. He's good friends with Himmler, the Führer's right-hand man. Used to sell that crackpot laying hens when he was just a chicken farmer. If you need a favor, ask, and I'll do my best to pay you back for your hospitality."

"I...thank you, Herr Muller," whispered the Rabbi, looking at his daughter and watching her play dollhouse with the German child, dread welling up in his chest like a balloon.

I should have packed Alica up and left that night, but I

didn't want to abandon my people. I thought that if and when Hitler came, it would be better if I was there to help, to cash in Herr Muller's favor for my community.

"And when they came...?"

I tried to get by at first, but it was hard. Our village was transformed into a ghetto, and Jews from all over the nation were crammed in. Food became scarce, everything became scarce. For me, for my congregation...for my daughter.

"Papa, look, I found an apple!"

The Rabbi was once again sitting in his study, but it looked completely different. The books and fineries had been stripped away, either stolen by the Nazis or sold for necessities. The Rabbi was scowling at an old medical tome, perhaps looking for a way to treat his patients when supplies were so scarce.

He looked up at his daughter. Alica, a few years older, looked too terrible to be smiling. Her hair was matted and filthy, her dress torn, her cheeks hollow and placid. Nevertheless, she smiled, holding up a half-eaten apple.

"An apple!" she cried happily. "I think one of the Germans threw it out before he finished. Do you wanna bite?"

"Alica..."

The Rabbi watched in despair as his pathetic, precious daughter bit into the apple, and Vilém prayed that he never felt as terrible about his own parenting skills. The horrible sensation that struck the Rabbi right then, the sensation that he was failing his daughter...panic and guilt weighed him down. It felt like there was a brick in his gut.

"Papa, why are you crying? It tastes fine, Papa!"

Alica insisted, offering the filthy fruit to her father. "Please have a bite, Papa…"

Tears blinded the Rabbi, and the memory faded into darkness.

That…that…seeing her do that, I knew I had to call in the favor…even if it meant kissing Himmler's bloody boots.

"Don't feel bad…she's your daughter…" Vilém said. "You had to protect her."

I had many obligations, boychik. To my daughter, to my congregation…I had hoped that Herr Muller's brother could help me take care of all of them. I was terribly naïve. Still…Herr Muller did what he could, and he wasn't lying when he said his brother had friends in high places.

"Come on, Jew. If you embarrass me, I'll kill you and then I'll kill my brother."

Vilém felt the Rabbi bite down on his tongue. The weary, starving Rabbi trudged behind a man who was almost identical to Herr Muller save for his relative youth and haggard appearance. Alois Muller marched through the Ghetto gates, and the Rabbi felt his heart flutter as he stepped out of the Ghetto for what must have been the first time in years.

"This way! You're lucky he's here, I would *not* have the patience to drag you all the way to Prague," Alois grunted, leading the Rabbi past several sneering SS soldiers, towards a small tent.

Before Vilém could even begin to wonder who "he" was, Alois entered the tent and the Rabbi followed at his heels. Vilém felt his heart somersault. Inside the tent was a gaggle of Nazis sitting around a table that boasted a map of the Ghetto. Towering above all the SS men was a familiar snake-like face.

"Heil Hitler, General Heydrich!" Alois barked, shoving his hand into the air.

"Fuck, not him…" muttered Vilém. Heydrich stood up, his already narrow eyes becoming even thinner as he scowled at the Rabbi. Vilém felt uncertainty rise in the Rabbi's chest, perhaps because he didn't know how to greet the Nazi General. Surely a Hitler-salute would be seen as an insult.

Heydrich grunted, and a teeny smirk played on the edge of his lips when he sensed the Jew's fear. "This is the one who is willing to cooperate?" he said, looking towards Alois. Vilém felt the urge to snicker but suppressed it. Heydrich's squeaky voice would never sound natural, especially when he was trying to be intimidating.

"Yes, Reichsprotektor," Alois said. "My brother said he was pliant. He knows German, and he is relatively cultured compared to the rest of the Jews in this area."

"Oh, that's not always a positive," Heydrich mused, folding his hands behind his back and approaching the Rabbi. He gazed down at the Doctor as though he were a cockroach that had just skittered onto the countertop. "The so-called *cultured* ones are the biggest problem. Our people are fooled by them, and they blend in too well."

His icy blue eyes scanned the Rabbi and he shrugged. "Well, this one's too obvious to fool anyone. You're a doctor, Jew?"

"He is, sir…"

"I wasn't talking to you, Muller," snapped Heydrich, nodding for the Rabbi to speak. The Rabbi felt his tongue twist itself into a knot, and for a moment he couldn't say a word.

"Yes…" he finally said, adding hastily, "Yes, Reich-sprotektor."

Heydrich, evidently pleased with the frightened correction, nodded. "While I normally wouldn't want to associate with someone who contributes to the longevity of the Jewish Race, I think you may have an appropriate mindset. Tell me, Jew: if a patient comes to you with an infected limb and you have no good options, what do you do to the limb?"

"Cut it off to save the body, Herr Reichsprotektor."

"Very good!" Heydrich said, clapping his gloved hands together. "You'll be used to making the sort of…decisions I need you to make. Come!" Heydrich pushed past the Jew, and his aggressive touch made the Rabbi squirm. The Doctor swallowed his pride and followed, no doubt thinking of Alica even as he trailed the Nazi like a loyal dog.

"You see," Heydrich said, rolling his eyes as every single SS man who saw him saluted like their lives depended on their gusto. "I want to show Hans Frank that my Czechs are far more productive than his Poles. I want this Ghetto to be the new Lodz. Smaller, obviously, but with just as much output. No waste whatsoever. It would please the Führer, and…"

He turned, smirking a wicked smirk. "It would give me an opportunity to be generous. You should know, Herr Doctor, that I'm fully aware that not all Jews *must* be eradicated. Some, perhaps, but the more pliant ones…the ones who demonstrate that they, unlike the rest, are not a threat to our people…"

"Herr Heydrich, we're not a threat!" the Rabbi interjected, perhaps seeing Heydrich's little proclamation as a sign that his mind could be changed. Heydrich turned, a blizzard spewing from his eyes, and the Rabbi timidly bowed his head.

"W-what I meant to say was…"

"Do not…" Heydrich hissed. "Do not speak unless you're told to, Jew. *That* is the behavior I'm talking about. Aberrant, rebellious, but…Jews who can learn their place, they may be granted certain privileges."

The Rabbi lifted a brow, but kept his lips shut. Heydrich observed his silence for a moment before smiling like a dog owner whose pet had just learned a new trick.

"You may speak your mind, Doctor," he said.

"What precisely do you want me to do, Herr Reich-sprotektor?"

"Simple! It's very hard to get the Jews to fall in line. They don't like to take orders from gentiles, they distrust us…not that I blame them. But it makes my job harder, and it means we waste time and resources…and it also means that Jews who may otherwise be productive and pliant suffer…"

He patted his sidearm. "So what we've done in Poland—and what I would like to start doing here—is we have a designated Jewish Council made up of obedient Jews, Jews who know their place and are willing to enforce our rules for the betterment of their people and ours. They make sure the Jews in the factories keep up with quotas, they make sure the weaker Jews who cannot work are not wasting valuable Ghetto resources…"

"Uhm…" the Rabbi started to say before covering his mouth, and Heydrich snickered.

"You're doing so well already!" the Hangman chirped. "Go on, Doctor."

"What would happen to those...weaker Jews, Herr Heydrich?"

"For now? Resettlement. But we're coming up with a more permanent solution." the Blonde Beast leaned down, his smirk vanishing. "Now listen, Herr Doctor, for you I won't use euphemisms: it will not be pleasant. Humane, of course, we Germans are well known for treating animals humanely. But not pleasant...no..."

Heydrich's eyes suddenly flitted upwards, as though he expected to see the eyes of God scowling down at him. Both the Rabbi and Vilém were surprised to see a flash of fear dart across the Hangman's face. Whatever he was looking for did not manifest, however, and with a relieved exhale, Heydrich continued.

"Don't harbor any childish illusions. Your community is sick, and the only way it will survive is via amputation. If you are not willing to assist in the operation, you may very well find yourself hacked off...you, and those you care for. Would you prefer to be a limb, Doctor?"

The Rabbi covered his mouth with his hands, shaking. He must have known before he even called in his favor that the Nazis were planning on a massive pogrom; Vilém didn't feel surprise course through the Doctor's body. Just guilt. Guilt and love, love for Alica. He inhaled deeply and made his Faustian bargain.

"I'll do what you want...if you can promise me that no child will be harmed."

"I can't promise that," Heydrich said, his voice becoming quiet, almost contemplative. "I can promise that my men will not choose who is to live and who is to die...within reason. You will be the head of the *Judenrat*, you will make those decisions, and you may spare whoever is most worthy of being spared. If you do this and you do it well, I will procure supplies and the Ghetto will flourish. If you do not...it will starve."

The Rabbi clutched at his heart, which hammered as though to protest. He ignored its pleas and bowed his head to the murderer.

"We'll be very productive, Reichsprotektor," he promised, and Heydrich beamed at his petty victory.

"Salute properly, please," the Butcher of Prague sneered. "You work for me now, I insist."

Revulsion boiled in the Rabbi's chest, but what very little pride he had clung to evaporated as he obeyed, raising one hand into the air and whispering, "Heil Hitler..."

The memory faded into darkness, and Vilém blurted out, "Do *not* feel bad about anything that *monster* made you do! He was *beyond* evil! He gave you false hope, he *lied* to you..."

No, he didn't. He never lied about anything. I accepted it...because I wanted to save Alica.

"She was your daughter! Of course you would kiss that fuckhead's boots if it meant saving her!"

Yes...and I did. I ran the Judenrat like a good little pet, and Heydrich...well, he always favored the carrot and stick method.

"Doctor!"

The Rabbi was being escorted out of the Ghetto, along with a small group of elderly men and women. The old Jews were pushed into the back of a gray truck, and the Rabbi watched, guilt throttling his heart.

But his focus was diverted to a motorcycle that roared to a halt close by. Heydrich, looking arrogant as ever, hopped off the vehicle and gestured for the Rabbi to come. Doctor Doubek skittered to the Blonde Beast's side.

"Look!" Heydrich said, gingerly prodding the motorcycle with the toe of his jackboot. "Runs well, and it was made in this Ghetto. Production has soared, and with far fewer instances of sabotage."

"My congregation trusts me," the Rabbi confessed. Heydrich looked like he might have laughed, but he refrained.

"I'm very pleased," said the Butcher of Prague. "Your Ghetto will receive double rations…"

Heydrich's high-pitched voice faded as the Rabbi heard a yelp of pain. He looked towards the trucks. An old woman had fallen trying to get on. Another man tried to stoop down and help her, but the Nazis smacked him with their batons.

"Move it, Jew! Step over it!" snapped one SS officer, and one by one the Jews were forced onto the truck, forced to trample the woman. She cried out over and over and the Rabbi…the Rabbi watched, he listened, he heard her screams and wanted so desperately to help her.

"Doctor!" But Heydrich's goat-like bleat, laced with ire at being ignored, broke through the haze. Heydrich looked at the fallen old woman, whose cries had finally been silenced. She was covered in blood, but the Rabbi could see her twitch. She was still breathing.

The Hangman rolled his eyes. "How typical…" he muttered, eyes flitting upwards once more. He leaned down, grunting as though he had been pushed, hovering above the Rabbi's shoulder.

"Doctor," he said. "I just said I'm giving your people extra rations and the Sabbath off. I think a 'thank you' is in order."

A Nazi walked over to the fallen woman, stepping on top of her and slamming the truck door shut. He knocked on the back of the van twice and it drove off, leaving the broken woman behind. The Nazi looked down, nudged her with his heel, then pulled out his gun.

"Well?" Heydrich growled. The Rabbi shut his eyes.

"Thank you, Herr Heydrich…" he whispered, and a gunshot echoed across the Ghetto.

When the Rabbi opened his eyes again, he found himself standing in the synagogue. The Jews were sitting cheek-to-jowl, some on the benches, some on the floor. Only the young and healthy remained. Some children played in the middle aisle. Alica was with them, throwing jacks across the wooden floor. She was much healthier than before: full rosy cheeks, clean clothes, washed hair…but her smile was gone.

My bargain with Heydrich seemed to…succeed for some time. We worked for the Nazis, none of us were deported except the old and sick…and I thought…I hoped we wouldn't have to sacrifice more. But one day Heydrich gave me a new order, a terrible order. He wanted more space in the Ghetto for more workers…more food for workers…and the children…

"Oh no…" whispered Vilém, watching through the Rabbi's tear-obscured eyes as he stood before the congregation.

"I come to you today with a heavy heart," he

announced. "For the past few weeks, our willingness to cooperate has allowed us relative prosperity…"

"Rabbi, my mother's gone!" one woman retorted. "I don't feel very prosperous!"

"My dear, your mother is much happier where she is, in another ghetto…have you not received a letter from her yet?" queried the Rabbi.

"I have, but…" the woman said, plucking a small postcard from her dress pocket and holding it up. "It feels…wrong, Rabbi, like it wasn't written by her hand. It's like…like someone else wrote it."

"Oh, my dear, please…" the Rabbi begged, guilt battering his spirit. "For all of their gusto, the Germans have not burned our synagogue. They're far more cultured than any other gentile force we have had to deal with in the past. Are you going to believe some wild conspiracy theory?"

"I…suppose not…" whispered the woman, sinking down into her seat and staring at the forged postcard.

Heydrich had it all planned out so well. He really was an evil genius. He made sure they signed a paper before they were shipped off to die, and then he had an entire team of prisoners write postcards to the living family members, to keep them calm and ignorant.

"Shitface," snarled Vilém, overwhelmed by the urge to drive over to Prague and kick Heydrich's ghost square in his ethereal face.

"I want to assure you," the Rabbi lied, every word tasting foul on his tongue. "Your mothers and fathers and grandparents are fine. The Reichsprotektor merely wants to turn our village into a model of productivity, and sadly that means we must be separated from our loved ones for some time, until we have reached our quotas. Life will get better! We will be reunited and the hard times will be a distant memory."

The congregation tensed, as though they had heard this speech one too many times and knew that a fresh deportation was about to begin.

"But we must continue to cooperate if we are to get through this as a community. Believe me, my people, I wish there were another way, but it is better to coop-erate than to rebel and die. And so...I must ask you to cooperate with me. I have received another order from Reichsprotektor Heydrich..."

"We've already deported all of our elders, there's nobody left to deport!" one Jew argued.

"Alas, there are many. Heydrich has ordered that one hundred children under the age of fourteen must be deported..."

The outcry was instant. Men shouted, women howled and held their children, and little boys and girls clung to their families, screaming that they didn't want to go. Alica stared at her father, eyes wide, mouth agape.

"Please! Please!" the Rabbi cried. "Your children will be taken to the same old-age ghetto as your elders, they will be given schooling and..."

"Why can't they get that here?!" one woman yelled, hugging her toddler to her breast.

"Any mother who does not wish to be separated from her child is welcome to go with them, though I do not recommend it as Herr Heydrich wants as many workers to remain here as possible!" the Rabbi said. "Herr Heydrich is plotting out a humane way for us to coexist, but the war is raging and he wants the Ghetto to be exclusively devoted to production! Your children will be fine, but we must obey the quota…"

"What about *your* daughter?!" one man shouted, pointing at Alica. The Rabbi's daughter winced as all eyes fell upon her. She looked up at her father, her head tilting inquisitively to the side, as though to silently ask, "Yes, what about me?"

"There will be a raffle, a fair raffle," the Rabbi announced. "One hundred names will be chosen out of a hat, excluding babies too young to be separated from their mothers. It will be fair, and my daughter's name will be in there as well. And if she is sent away, I will not shed a tear. I promise you, our children will be safe! They will be safer at the other ghetto than they will be here! If my daughter's name is called, God be blessed!"

The congregation, somewhat calmed by the Rabbi's proclamation of equality, let their screams morph into whispers, clinging to their babies, their eyes flitting between Doctor Doubek and Alica. The Rabbi's daughter smiled at her father, but it wasn't the same sunny smile she had once possessed. It was a half-smile, chillingly similar to Heydrich's. A smile that spelled trouble.

The Rabbi blinked, and the memory shifted even as the location stayed the same. The Jews were sitting in the synagogue, but a few fresh faces had joined the crowd. Nazi guards stood by the exit, their eyes trained on the Rabbi, who stood before the frightened congregation, clutching a hat filled with little slips of paper. He glanced at his daughter, who was sitting up front, leaning forward as though she were at a magic show and he was about to pull a rabbit from the hat.

37

"Please stay calm..." the Rabbi begged the Jews before him as he reached in and chose the first paper. He unfolded it.

Alica Doubek

He bit his lip, but didn't hesitate for one moment. "Chaim Nagel."

Chaim's mother screamed. The boy cried and clung to her. His father stood up, prepared to fight for his son, but a Nazi smacked him with a baton and grabbed the child, yanking him out of the synagogue. His screams rung in the Rabbi's ears.

Doctor Doubek tore up his daughter's name and pulled out another paper.

Alica Doubek

His eyes widened and he stole a glance at his daughter. Her little hands were balled into fists, clutching the ribbon on her dress. There was a dare in her eyes.

"Rivka Orten..."

And on and on it went, the Rabbi pulling out his daughter's name one hundred times, the Rabbi lying one hundred times, Alica's smile dying one hundred times as one hundred families were destroyed.

When they were done, Alica stood, tears in her eyes, and ran from the synagogue. The Rabbi's heart almost stopped, and he moved without a single thought, barreling past furious, mourning parents and chasing his distraught daughter into the street.

Alica was watching as the other children were tossed onto the trucks. She watched as they were driven off, driven to their deaths. She watched, and Vilém saw a piece of her wither away right then. The sunshine in her soul vanished with her friends.

"Alica, come…" the Rabbi begged, grabbing her arm. She pulled away.

"Don't touch me!" she shrieked, shoving him and running away. He cursed and followed her all the way back to their home.

"Alica!" he gasped as he burst into their house, collapsing to his knees and trying to catch his breath. She was standing in the living room, hugging one hundred pieces of paper. She tossed them in her father's face and he winced as the names of all the Jewish children fell on him like snow.

"You…you replaced the papers, then…why?" the Rabbi asked. Alica, who now truly looked like the furious Ms. Doubek that Vilém knew too well, snarled.

"You're a liar and a hypocrite!" she accused. "You've been working with the Nazis all this time and lying for them! And if you lied about sending me off, that means they're gonna die!"

Alica choked, tears streaming down her face as she looked at the papers covering her living room floor. "You just murdered all my friends…"

"Alica, I didn't murder them, please, listen…" the Rabbi begged, crawling towards his daughter and reaching out to hold her face in his hands. "They would have killed every single one of us, they would have killed you too…"

"What happened to sit and do nothing, huh?" Alica screeched, slapping his hands away. She grabbed the corner of his *tallit* prayer scarf and shoved it in front of his eyes. "What about this? What about the Talmud and the Torah? What about God's laws? What about everything you ever told me?"

"Alica!" the Rabbi yelped as she pulled the holy garment right off of him and tossed it to the ground.

"It was all just a lie wasn't it? Just a lie to make me feel better about Mother and everything else in this stupid, horrible world!"

"Alica, it wasn't all a lie, this is...our people have dealt with such cruelty before..."

"Our people have never *betrayed* each other!" Alica screamed. "Our people didn't sacrifice children to Molech! Our Rabbis didn't *lie* to us! Our Rabbis were not selfish *traitors!*"

"Alica, please! I love God, and I love our people, but I love you more!" the Rabbi cried, standing up and trying to put a hand on his child's shoulder.

"Get away from me, I hate you!" Alica screamed. She ran up the stairs and slammed her bedroom door shut. The Rabbi, sobbing, knelt on the names of the children he had damned, and Vilém hoped to never feel the way Doctor Doubek did right then.

Tears filled his eyes, blinding him, and...

"Doctor?"

A familiar voice spoke in an unfamiliar tone as a new memory formed. The Doctor was sitting in front of Heydrich, who had made himself at home in the Rabbi's living room. The Hangman of Prague was sitting on the couch and clutching a folder labeled *"Ghetto 15 Output."* He must have been so pleased with Rabbi Doubek's cooperation that he had stopped by for a house call.

The Rabbi hastily blinked away his tears and rigidly stood at attention. Heydrich let out a noise like a teenager that had just been spoken to like a toddler.

"Oh, for Heaven's sake, enough of this dance!" huffed the Blonde Beast. "Just talk!"

Heydrich winced as though the invisible hand of Hitler had just smacked him for straying even slightly from Nazi protocol, but he seemed to recover quickly and waved for the Rabbi to speak. Vilém felt a lump of hesitation form in the Rabbi's throat as his mind buzzed with potential excuses, but he decided to tell the truth.

"Some of my daughter's friends were deported and she...put two and two together, Herr Reichsprotektor."

"Ah. Clever girl. More clever than half of Europe...or maybe just brave enough to speak the obvious."

"She's...upset with me for cooperating with you, Reichsprotektor. She thinks it is a betrayal of my religious values."

Heydrich gave the Rabbi a studious look, as though he were a rat that had just performed a feat of acrobatics.

"Is it?" the Butcher asked.

"...I...suppose," the Rabbi whispered.

Heydrich leaned forward and pulled back one end of the Newton's Cradle that still rested on the coffee table. His light blue eyes flitted back and forth as the balls clicked and clacked against one another, sending the metal orbs at the ends of the cradle flying.

"It seems your role as a doctor and a Rabbi are in conflict," Heydrich observed, keeping his eyes fixed on the silver cradle.

"She said she hates me," sighed the Rabbi. "Even after I did all of this for her."

Heydrich's thin eyes widened. Vilém saw his hand

flit towards his back pocket. Perhaps he had his wallet there. Perhaps he had a picture of Klaus inside. Perhaps the Nazi was recalling his own son's words. Heydrich reached forward and cupped the clacking Newton's Cradle with both hands, forcing it to become still once more.

"I know how that feels…" the Hangman whispered, slowly leaning back, staring at the still-trembling Newton's Cradle. Vilém almost couldn't believe his ears when he heard empathy in the Nazi's tone. Heydrich winced again, as though an unseeable force had punished him once more for daring to sympathize with a Jew. He scowled upwards, and the possibly-imaginary being that kept striking him seemed to slacken its grip on his soul.

"Children are far too simple and innocent for their own good," he said, staring at the multiple distorted little Reinhard Heydrichs that the orbs of the Newton's Cradle reflected. "They so rarely recognize that occasionally…painful and terrible as it may be…we must…do things that are wrong so they can be safe…"

He glanced down at his own gloved hand and shook his head, looking up at the Rabbi with a small, genuine smile.

"I'll continue to give you and your child what you deserve," Heydrich vowed. "You're very different from the rest of the Jews, Doctor. Almost human. In fact…I don't think we're very different at all."

Heydrich winced again, as though that confession had hurt his very soul, and with a brusque farewell he grabbed his things and scurried out of the Rabbi's home.

"So…" Alica's voice drifted into the Rabbi's ear. He looked towards the staircase. Alica was there, her hair unbrushed, frowning deeply.

"Not so different," she sneered. "I guess you're not."

She turned around and marched back upstairs, and the Rabbi, weighted down by guilt and disgust, collapsed onto the couch, covering his face with his hands as though he wanted to hide from the very face of God.

So…still think I should get my own exhibit?

Vilém, who had been prepared for a lot but certainly not this sort of moral dilemma, huffed. "This is *not* your fault, Rabbi! I'm no historian, but I've read enough to know that yarn Heydrich spun about sparing *some* Jews was bull. He lied to you…"

And I lied to my people.

"What else were you supposed to do? Sit and die?"

That is what the Talmud instructs. That is what I spent my life preaching.

"I'm not a Jew, but I don't think God would be angry at someone who genuinely tried to save lives."

By damning others to death…

"Rabbi, they were all dead from the moment the Nazis marched into Czechoslovakia!" Vilém argued. "Perhaps your actions saved a few of them…"

And perhaps not. Perhaps they would have escaped, lived. Perhaps I should have told my people to fight back.

"With what, sticks and stones?" Vilém exclaimed. "You had nothing, you were helpless! You shouldn't have *had* to even *consider* fighting back against an army! Rabbi, there is no shame in making mistakes when there's a gun pointed at your head!"

Perhaps not, but there is shame in shoving someone else in front of the bullet.

"Maybe, but shoving someone else in front of your child...I don't know, Rabbi," Vilém sighed. "I'm not even a dad yet, but I feel like I'd commit a thousand sins so my kid could live. I'd do a million terrible things..."

Well, that's precisely what Heydrich thought he was doing. A million terrible things. Six million, more specifically.

"Well, he can think he was doing the right thing as much as he wants, but he wasn't, and he had plenty of opportunities to see that! You weren't given the same choices he was! Don't compare yourself to him!" Vilém snapped.

I truly appreciate your words, Vilém. Nonetheless, can you blame Alica for despising me?

"Well..." muttered Vilém. "I can't pretend like I've ever been in her shoes. The only thing me and my old man ever really argued about was my curfew, and I said I hated him too...but I didn't. I bet she doesn't either. She's just...upset."

She has a right to be. I really tried to protect her, but I failed.

"Failed? She's alive!"

Alive, certainly, but that doesn't mean I didn't fail her. That conversation with Heydrich was the last one we had before he was assassinated. Suddenly, our terrible benefactor was gone and Hitler was seething. Hitler demanded reprisals, and we were swept up. My daughter, what was left of our congregation, and myself.

"And that's how you got to the Camp?"

Correct. But fortunately, once we arrived and the Selection started, the Nazis asked for doctors to step out of line. And there I was again, making a bargain with a demon.

"This is her?"

"Yes, Herr Kommandant."

"Get off of me!" Alica demanded, trying and failing to free herself from the grasp of the Nazi guard who dragged her into a familiar office. Vilém grunted. Kommandant Gerber's office again. The Kommandant sat at his desk, as usual, though all aggravation and arrogance had abandoned him. He wore a neutral expression as he allowed his bright blue eyes to dart from Alica to the Doctor, finally settling on the trembling Rabbi.

"So..." sighed the Kommandant, standing up. "We have an agreement, then."

"Where's the boy?" the Doctor asked.

"He has his own nursery," the Kommandant said, crossing his arms behind his back and sauntering towards the window. "You will stay in the infirmary. You'll be on call at all times. If Martin has an accident, you will drop everything to take care of him."

"And my daughter...?" the Rabbi said. Alica snarled.

"I can't believe you're making *another* deal with them!" she cried.

"Shut her up, please, I can't handle the screeching," snapped the Kommandant, and his soldier covered the girl's mouth with his hand. The Rabbi didn't seem to notice—or if he did, he forced himself to ignore it—but Vilém saw a wolf-like smirk form on the Nazi's face as he muffled the girl's cries, as if this was a familiar, pleasant motion.

"Fuckhead," whispered Vilém, but the Kommandant spoke again before Vilém could let out any more curses.

"I would offer your daughter the spare room, but

we've converted it into a developing room," he said, gesturing to the camera that rested on his desk. "And I already have a Jewess staying there. Besides, your daughter's...feisty. I don't think I want her near Martin."

Alica kicked and let out a muffled howl.

"My point precisely," the Kommandant said, flourishing his hand to indicate the thrashing girl. "She's...how old now?"

"Thirteen, Kommandant."

"Thirteen, fine," the Kommandant said, jabbing his thumb towards the window, gesturing to Barrack Two. "She'd normally be placed in the children's barrack, but the women's barrack will be safer. I'll give my men orders not to touch her, and she can have double rations under-the-table. I can't offer much more: too much favoritism will make her a target to the other prisoners. We've had some...race-mixing difficulties with some soldiers and believe me...the Jewesses in those cases never fared well."

The Rabbi shuddered and glanced at Alica. She looked at him with fire in her eyes, as though he was nothing more than another Nazi, no better than the Kommandant.

"Very well, Herr Kommandant," Doctor Doubek agreed. "As long as she's safe and I get a chance to see her."

"Good, good!" the Kommandant said. "Then take the Jewess to Barrack Two and be sure to give her a special armband so the rest of the men know not to touch her."

"Yes, sir," the Nazi guard snickered, and with that he carried the writhing Alica Doubek out of the office, slamming the door behind him.

And well...you sort of know what happened after that. I lived in the infirmary. I worked for Little Martin Gerber...a sweet boy. He didn't speak much, but believe it or not, he was a Jew by faith.

"You're kidding!" Vilém cried. "I thought he was a Czech!"

Half Czech, half German, and I suspect his mother was a convert to Judaism. For some reason—and Martin never told me why, maybe even he didn't know—but for some reason, the Kommandant was determined to mold Martin into a good little Nazi. Gerber made it clear to me that if I taught the boy about Judaism or encouraged him to be a Jew, I would be in trouble.

"And...?"

Well...Martin was very persuasive.

"Doctor Rabbi, do you know what day it is?"

"It's hard to keep track of the days, boychik, please hold still..." The Rabbi was tending to Little Martin, who was pale as a corpse save for his knee, which boasted a huge, ugly black bruise.

"It's Yom Kippur!" the boy announced. The Rabbi felt his heart plummet. He winced when the child's stomach snarled.

"Boychik, you will get us both in trouble. You *must* eat. Did you injure yourself on purpose again?" whispered the Rabbi. Little Martin smiled, and something about that smile made Vilém's heart flutter.

"Maybe," the child said cheekily. "I wanted to sing Kol Nidre."

"I have a terrible voice, boychik. Please do not bump yourself on purpose, you could die."

"Fine," huffed Martin, glowering at the bandage the

47

Rabbi wrapped around his bruised leg. "Then the Kommandant could get a new pet."

"You really should call him Father, boychik, you know he..."

"He's not my father, I don't have a father!" the boy insisted. Martin's eyes shifted to the ceiling and he added, "Except God. But...maybe He's gone too."

The Rabbi felt a rush of agreement, followed by a stab of shame for his own lack of faith. He gently patted the boy's cheek. "Boychik, don't speak that way. One day we will be free and you will find your papa."

Martin let out a shuddering breath, as though the mere mention of his biological father lit a fire in his belly. He slowly shook his head and muttered, "I just wanna sing Kol Nidre...please, Doctor Rabbi?"

The Rabbi's eyes darted anxiously to the door, as though he expected the Kommandant to burst in at any moment and execute him for merely entertaining the notion. He looked up at the white ceiling, waiting for a divine sign that didn't come.

He bit his lip, and a rebellious spirit took hold of him as he pulled the boy into a hug and sang in his ear, so quietly that only God could have heard.

"Kol Nidre...Ve'esarei...Ush'vuei..."

How could I refuse? My daughter despised me, but Martin still looked to me as a man of God, as a savior, as a hero...to the point where he trusted me when he came across a real hero.

"Doctor Rabbi!"

Vilém watched with fascination as a familiar memory played out, this time from the Doctor's point of view: Little Martin burst in with Joseph Klammer in tow,

Joseph revealed little Daniel Svoboda, Klammer and the Rabbi traded vague explanations.

It was strange, to feel it all in another body, to see it all with a new pair of eyes. In Joseph's memory, the Rabbi had seemed so calm. In reality, a war raged within the Doctor's soul as he looked down at Danny. Fear pulled him towards the Kommandant's office. He would probably be rewarded for turning the traitorous Nazi in. He would be known as a good, obedient Jew who knew his place. He would be safe. His daughter would be safe.

But guilt, guilt for all the children he had already betrayed, forced him to proclaim that he would hide the boy.

And for once, I didn't betray my people. I let little Danny stay in the infirmary. Thankfully, the Kommandant let me be, and Fido the Spy never intervened.

"Iveta wasn't a spy, and Daniel's my great-uncle," Vilém said. "You saved him."

Klammer saved him. I just didn't betray him the way I betrayed everyone else.

"Did Alica know?"

She didn't. Martin usually brought Danny food, but sometimes he just couldn't get us anything, not without making the Kommandant suspicious. When that happened, I had to split my rations with Daniel. If Alica had known, she would have given him her food as well. I didn't want her to go without, but...she often did.

"Alica, sunshine, you're thin." A new memory formed, so dark that it took a moment for Vilém to realize it: the Rabbi was inside the women's barrack, sitting on a straw-covered bunk beside his daughter.

If Alica was getting special privileges, it was hard to

tell. She looked just as emaciated, just as tired, and just as hopeless as the rest of the women. The only difference was that her head hadn't been shaved.

She played with her hair, picking at the mats, trying to loosen the knots.

"Alica, do you need a comb?" the Rabbi asked. The girl pretended as though she couldn't hear him, staring at her lap, her eyes empty. Vilém could barely tell that this was the same girl who had once possessed a blindingly sunny smile.

"Alic…"

"I don't have anyone to look pretty for," Alica hissed, tugging a knot out of her hair and wincing from the pain. The Rabbi bit his lip.

"Have the guards been…hurting you?"

"Who cares?" she whispered.

"You know I care, I…"

"It makes no difference. If they don't hurt me, they hurt another girl in Barrack Two."

"Have you been giving your rations to the other women in the barrack, Alica?"

Alica didn't answer, but her picking at her hair became frantic. A silent "yes."

"Alica, my brave girl, you're very sweet, but you must think of yourself first. An extra bite offered to everyone else will do them no good, it will not save their lives, but it will cost you yours."

"You don't understand anything," Alica insisted, hugging her knees to her chest and lying down, turning away from her father. "I'm tired."

"All right, but please, if you have something to tell me, just…I'll do whatever I can to help you."

"I know you will..." Alica whispered, and it sounded as though knowing that made her ill. The Rabbi stood above his daughter, and Vilém felt a tug in the Doctor's chest. The Rabbi wanted to kiss his daughter goodbye, but cowardice made him flee from the barrack before he could dare.

A familiar face was waiting outside Barrack Two: none other than Private Helmut Schwartz. Vilém chuckled. Then that meant...

The Rabbi looked up and saw a distressed Joseph Klammer exit Barrack Three. Ah, familiarity.

"Hello, Sergeant!" the Rabbi cried, and again the same memory played out: Joseph took the Rabbi from Schwartz and started leading him back towards Barrack One. The Pit started burning...the smell made the Rabbi's gut writhe.

"That could be Danny..." the Rabbi said. "In a week, it will be Samuel. What is the difference? Why save one and damn another?"

Vilém was surprised how different this conversation felt from the Rabbi's point of view. In Joseph's mind, the holy man had been offering him a moral lesson. But Vilém felt bitterness settle on the Rabbi's tongue and he realized that Doctor Doubek was talking to himself more than he was talking to Joseph.

"Selfishness, Rabbi..." Joseph said, and Vilém felt empathy rise up in the Rabbi's chest.

"At least *you're* honest," the Rabbi sighed, and even as Joseph tried to cover his nose, the Rabbi inhaled deeply, fanning the flames of his guilt, reminding himself of the fate he had consigned so many Jewish babies to.

You see now? Joseph didn't understand one bit. He thought he was the one who needed redemption.

"Joseph's a hero, but he *did* kill people before he figured out that the Nazi worldview was bullshit," Vilém said. "You made mistakes, but you saved Danny...and you saved the rest of the Jews, you helped Joseph!"

Ah, yes, the Freedom Train. Well, Joseph was very convincing. He told me that if I didn't help him, all the women in Barrack Two would perish, including my daughter. At first, I thought my daughter might be spared...we did have our deal, the Kommandant and I.

"But...?"

But the Kommandant never said a word about the deportation. Never warned me, never did anything to save my daughter. Perhaps he forgot all about her. I have a feeling he wanted to replace me, though: Martin had been acting like a good little Nazi, perhaps Gerber decided to get him a less undesirable doctor. Regardless, my daughter was evidently going to be treated just like every other Jew. She was going to die...and I couldn't let that happen. I let Sergeant Klammer think I did it for my people, but I actually did it for her.

"You're saving her life, Doctor." They were back in the infirmary, the day before the Freedom Train left the station. Joseph placed a hand on the Rabbi's shoulder. The Rabbi looked into the young Aryan's eyes and saw a familiar flame, a flame of guilt burning in Klammer's irises.

"You as well..." Doctor Doubek said, forcing his eyes to burrow into Joseph's, perhaps hoping that Klammer would see the inferno of guilt in the Rabbi's soul and realize that he was the better man. "God be with you, Joseph."

"Just this once…" Joseph sighed. He said his farewells to the children and scurried off to Barrack Three. As soon as he was gone, Little Martin dropped the ratty toy cat he was holding and ran to Danny, planting a determined kiss on the toddler's cheek.

"I'm not staying!" Little Martin vowed. The Rabbi winced.

"Martin…"

"I'm not staying! I hate Gerber! I want to go with you and Danny!" Martin yelped, pointing to the door and adding, "The little spy's gone now, so he won't notice I'm gone if I leave last-minute!"

"Martin!" the Rabbi hissed, shushing Danny as the toddler squealed joyously at the notion of his friend coming along and playing the quiet game. "Martin, I know you've been through a lot, but if you leave, the Kommandant may hunt us down to the ends of the earth…"

"I know it's selfish, Rabbi, but I can't stand it anymore!" Martin cried. "I'd rather die a Jew than live like this for another second! I hate this! I'm so sorry, but please let me be selfish! Please let me come with you! Please…it's my birthday!"

The Rabbi almost laughed at the boy's invocation of his not-birthday, but Little Martin wasn't joking. He fell at the Doctor's feet, his brilliant eyes wide and pleading, tears cascading down his cheeks. Danny started crying, reaching for Martin.

"No leave! No!" Danny cried. The Rabbi's ears buzzed, the screams and pleas of both children summoning the ghosts of old sins.

"All right…all right, you can come, but you must

disguise yourself..." the Rabbi said, finally allowing an authentic smile to bloom on his face as the two boys shrieked with happiness and hugged one another.

How could I refuse? Those boys loved each other, and after everything he went through, Martin had more of a right to be selfish than I did. He deserved to be free, to be a Jew, to keep that little spark of innocence alive. The day came and...haha! Well, he definitely disguised himself.

"Doctor Rabbi, look!"

A hectic memory formed. Jews, unaware that they would be free in a few hours, wailed and tried to say their last goodbyes to their loved ones as the Nazis shoved them onto the Auschwitz Train. The Rabbi had been holding a half-asleep Danny and staring at the top of the train. Schwartz and a few others were getting into position atop the cattle cars. Klammer was nowhere to be seen.

The Rabbi looked down at Little Martin and almost burst into laughter. The boy had shorn his curly blonde locks and stolen a dress. Vilém chuckled. He must have snatched one of Iveta's spares some time ago, just in case he was eventually given this kind of opportunity.

"See? I look like a girl!" Martin whispered, his eyes dancing as he ran a hand over the stubble on his head. "I look like all the other Jews!"

He sounded so happy. The little boy had been stripped of his Jewishness for so long that being shaved, dirty, and despised made him giddy. He hadn't been lying when he said that he would rather die as a Jew than keep living as the Kommandant's project.

"Ah, ah!" Little Daniel woke up and saw his cross-dressing friend, recognizing his voice. The toddler reached down, softly crying for Martin.

"Give him to me," Martin volunteered. "I can take him to his papa. You find Alica and we'll all meet after this is over."

"Ah...yes, after..." mumbled the Rabbi. He felt his heart sink as he gazed at the cheerfully smiling and terribly ignorant little boy. He knelt before Martin, setting little Daniel on his back and kissing the older boy's almost-bald head.

"Go, and God bless you. If anything happens to me, find my daughter. She'll take care of you."

"Nothing will happen to you, Rabbi! God's watching!" Martin said confidently. "This is a mitzvah, He'll protect you!"

"Of course He will..." the Rabbi whispered. He kissed both boys once more and watched as Martin piggy-backed Daniel towards the crowd of former Barrack Three occupants.

I never saw him again. I hope he stayed safe. He was a good boy.

"I'll look into him," Vilém vowed. "Maybe Ms. Doubek knows where he went and—UNGH!"

All of a sudden, an invisible force assaulted Vilém. Not a mere kick to the gut: it felt like someone had jabbed their thumbs right into his eyes. He fell back into Barrack Two, writhing on the wooden floor, clutching his face.

"Fuck, fuck, fuck!" he yelped, and for a few moments he feared that the wicked spirit had blinded him, but slowly he managed to open his eyes a sliver. He was barely able to see, but he knew he still had his sight, and that was enough to keep him from rushing to the hospital. He reached out and touched the panel once more, shutting his injured eyes.

Mr. Rehor, are you all right? You have a black eye...you have two black eyes! And that presence...

"Kommandant Gerber?" Vilém assumed.

I'd recognize that...coldness anywhere. It seems he still holds a grudge. I suppose I did steal his "son."

"And it looks like he's lashing out at me," Vilém huffed.

You are bringing up some old wounds, I suppose. Perhaps he was content so long as we were all stuck here together. I doubt he wants to be alone in his misery.

"Too bad," Vilém grunted. "Let's finish this. Tell me what happened with Ms. Doubek."

Vilém, you're hurt, and he may come back...and I don't want anyone else getting hurt on my account.

"And I don't want that shithead Gerber to win," Vilém countered. "Tell me what happened, Rabbi, please."

Very well, but then you have to go to the hospital. If you want me to have peace, that won't happen if you go blind. You deserve to see your baby.

Vilém smiled fondly, and the thought of his future child granted him a surge of strength. He was going to be a dad. He was going to have a baby. He needed to be good, to be brave, to be the sort of man his child could look at with adoring eyes.

Well...where were we? Oh, yes...

"Alica!"

Rabbi Doubek spotted his daughter among the frightened women: easy enough since she was the only one who still had her hair. In one swift motion, he grabbed her and wrapped Danny's blanket around her head.

"Stop! What are you doing?" she huffed.

"You mustn't let them see you," he whispered, pulling his daughter close. She tried to wriggle away, but sacrificing her double rations had made her weak.

"I'm going with everyone else!" she argued. "Enough deals!"

"Enough deals," the Rabbi agreed. "We're leaving with the others. I'm going too."

Alica ceased her struggling, looking up at her father with inquisitiveness. Before she could even open her mouth to question him, however, a familiar voice snapped at the father and daughter.

"Move it, Jews!" Joseph Klammer appeared behind them, grabbing the Rabbi and Alica. Alica froze when the man laid a hand on her, and the Rabbi, seeing his daughter's panic, whispered to Joseph.

"Gentle, please, my friend," he begged. Alica shot a glare at her father.

"No more deals," she spat, dragging her feet as Joseph, feigning forcefulness, led them to the train and opened the rearmost cattle car.

"Hey, Sergeant Klammer, it's crowded back there!" one of the Nazis on top of the train warned. Joseph smiled up at him.

"Five Marks says I can fit them both in!" he dared, and Vilém saw the bitterness in the reformed Nazi's eyes.

"You're on!" laughed Joseph's "comrade." Joseph

57

threw Alica in first, then her father, making sure he would be near the door.

"Wait until we're far…" Joseph whispered, sliding the door shut and pretending to lock it.

"There! Five Marks, Dietrich!" he cried, and the Rabbi heard him climb on top of the train.

"Goddammit," hissed the losing Nazi. "Fucking Jews…"

"Don't be mad, Dietrich," Schwartz chuckled. "You can get even when we get to Auschwitz."

"Auschwitz…" whispered Alica. The Rabbi tried to look down at his daughter, but the train car was so crowded that he couldn't even turn to face her. He reached out and put a hand on top of her head. She pushed him away.

"Get off," she hissed. The train took off with a roar and the Jews inside cried out in fear.

"Can I sit, please?" one exhausted Jew beside the Rabbi begged.

"Nobody can sit!" another prisoner whimpered.

"Lean against me," the Rabbi offered. "Stay strong."

"Bless you…" the man sighed, leaning his body against the Rabbi. Alica grunted. For what felt like an eternity, but must have only been an hour at most, they chugged along. The Rabbi peeked through the holes in the wooden cattle car, making sure that the Camp had disappeared into the distance.

"Sir, please stand!" Doctor Doubek begged the exhausted Jew who was leaning his scant weight against him.

"I can't, sir…" the Jew moaned.

"Please, somebody take him!" the Rabbi cried. "We're going to escape! We're not going to Auschwitz!"

"What...?" muttered Alica as another Jew, eager to help the Rabbi free his people, let the ill prisoner lean against him.

"Alica, my dear, I love you," Doctor Doubek cried, forcing his body to contort so he could see his daughter one last time. "Smile, please, sunshine..."

Her face, partially concealed by the darkness, glowed with confusion for a moment before the scowl that Vilém knew her for conquered her countenance.

"I don't want to," she said. "I don't trust you."

Sorrow drowned the Rabbi's soul. He reached out, touched her cheek, and his hand burned when she pulled away. The final rejection solidified his will to go, and without the slightest bit of hesitation, he threw open the door and jumped.

Alica evidently hadn't been expecting that. "Papa!" she shrieked, but adrenaline didn't allow him to look back at her. He ran, ran, ran...

BAM!

A bullet struck him in the chest. It hurt, but not worse than Alica's hatred. He fell to the dirt, barely able to raise his head enough to look up, barely able to hear the cries of the Nazis as Joseph shot them in the back.

All he heard was Alica, screaming. "PAPA!"

He saw the train speed off, he saw it vanish...a small fleck of happiness settled on his soul. Not enough to suppress the woe of knowing that his daughter despised him, but enough that he could press his face into the dirt and let out a satisfied sigh. She hated him, but she was safe. She would live.

He was alone. With only himself, the seemingly dead Nazis, and whatever God was watching over him.

"Sh'ma...Yisrael..." he tried, even as the life drained from him, to give an almost empty proclamation of his faith, but he couldn't. He wasn't strong enough.

He lay there, alone, silent, and eventually, everything went dark.

It was a slow death, and Vilém hoped that he wouldn't die that way. He pulled his hands away from the panel and opened his injured eyes.

A face, once one in a hundred, emerged from the crowd in the picture he had been touching. A face that had once made the Rabbi's heart sing, a face that had refused to smile for him. Alica Doubek, barely a dot among the Jews, sat in the back of Barrack Two, staring at the camera, her face drooping like a dead flower.

"Oh, Rabbi..." whispered Vilém. He shut his eyes again and touched the image of little Alica.

I miss her smile...but I know I don't deserve it. She was right about me. I was a fool...and a traitor.

"Depends on the definition of 'traitor,'" Vilém argued. "As far as I know, a man's first obligation is to his child. Above everything else. Not all selfishness is evil, and if protecting your child is selfishness, then everyone is selfish. Joseph only did what he did because he loved Sam, you did what you did because you loved your daughter..."

And that makes it all right?

"I don't know, Rabbi!" huffed Vilém. "I'm not God! And I'm not you, either! God willing, I'll never find myself in the same position you found yourself in...and if I do, I don't know what I'd do! A thousand children for my child? I don't know...maybe it is wrong, maybe it is evil, but...well, I'm not casting stones. It's not my place. How can I damn you for making an impossible choice? And anyone who would call you a monster, they have no right! And that includes Ms. Doubek!"

Alica suffered horribly...

"Alica was a kid. She didn't have to make the same choices you did. What if she had been forced to choose between her friend and a stranger? Or choose between letting you live or letting a hundred strangers live? Yes, the choice you made was against your religious laws, but if I remember the Bible correctly, even great men sin. The greater the man, the greater the sin. David!"

He clapped his hands together. "King David! He let a man die, he knowingly sent a man to die for horribly selfish reasons, for reasons far worse than what you did, and God still gave him a kingdom!"

I appreciate that you're trying to comfort me with my faith, Vilém, but...I'm not so sure about those stories anymore.

"Real or not, stories have a point, and the point is that even godly men can be hypocrites. Life is more than just...following rules. I can see why Alica didn't put you in an exhibit...maybe you don't deserve an exhibit. But you deserve to see your daughter's smile..."

Vilém shakily stood up, announcing confidently, "And I think I know how to revive it."

Alica Doubek was not in a good mood, which was not in and of itself unusual. Alica Doubek was rarely in

ELYSE HOFFMAN

a good mood. Even when she was, even when everything was going perfectly, even when none of her employees were calling her "Kommandant" behind her back, even when dreadful little teenagers weren't disrespecting the dead...even then, she would refuse to show it. Her smile was reserved for...well, nobody. She had never found anyone worthy enough. If her father had not deserved it, nobody did.

Least of all Vilém Rehor, who was working off the fumes of her patience. That irresponsible borderline-criminal had given her so many dreadful days and nights. The thought that he was going to have a child soon made Alica fear for the human race. One Vilém was too many—future generations didn't need to deal with his defective genetics.

She almost had to admire his determination to disobey her. She brought up her unwillingness to give him paternity leave, and he managed to wound both his eyes and secure paid time off for workplace injuries. She assumed he was lounging in bed with his fiancée, eating candy and being babied by Ilona Sladký.

She was surprised, then, when she entered her office one day and found a note sitting on her desk, written in Vilém's barely-legible handwriting.

Please meet me in Barrack Two after closing.

She grunted, but her annoyance gave way to curiosity. Vilém was a frustratingly strange character, but even when attempting to look at the world from his brain-dead point of view, she couldn't think of one reason he would want to see her after dark. She almost chuckled as the notion of assault flashed through her mind. Maybe once upon a time, but thankfully she

62

wasn't pretty enough to worry about such things anymore.

Her frown deepened. At least she hoped that was the case.

Nevertheless, for as much as she didn't like Vilém, she thought he was stupid, not evil. She decided to oblige. Maybe he would finally give her a good excuse to fire him.

The day ended and she sent Vilém's replacement on a wild goose chase through the former guards' barracks. Ostensibly because she had seen a small child run that way, but really because she didn't want anyone to interrupt her verbal beating of Vilém Rehor. She grabbed a thick metal pointer just in case words weren't enough and a physical beating was required.

She marched into Barrack Two, which by now was too familiar to trigger any unpleasant memories. She found her employee sitting on the floor in front of a laptop, struggling to plug a small speaker into the device.

"Rehor, you're supposed to be on leave," Alica snapped. Vilém looked over his shoulder, showing off his two swollen eyes and a small smile.

"Oh, hello," he said, finally managing to plug the speaker in. "I figured it was about a fifty-fifty shot, you showing up. Glad you made this easy."

"Made *what* easy, Rehor?" huffed Alica, crossing her arms over her chest. "I'm not in the mood for this, I've been here all day."

"You're not running home to anyone, Ms. Doubek," Vilém sighed, and Alica felt a tsunami of fury crash over her.

"How dare you?" she snarled. "You have a lot of nerve, barging in, staying here *illegally* after hours, and then insulting me right to my face! You've gotten away with a lot of shit, Rehor, but I will not tolerate —!"

But Vilém pressed a button on the laptop, drowning her rant out with a song. A familiar song. A song she had tried her hardest to never hear again.

"Smile, darn ya' smile!
You know this great world is a good world after all…"

For a moment they stood there, Alica frozen, Vilém swaying slightly to the tune. He let it play for long enough that she knew without a doubt it was *that* song. The song she had broken the radio to. The song she had danced to when she still had a smile.

"Do you believe in ghosts, Ms. Doubek?" Vilém asked. She was so shocked that she could barely shake her head and force a scowl back onto her face.

"I don't believe in anything," she proclaimed.

"Not even love?"

Doubek rolled her eyes. "What is this, a fucking Disney film? I hope you're not trying to…"

"Not that kind of love, ma'am. The parent kind. The kind that would make someone do foolish, terrible things."

Alica's heart, which she had purposefully encased in frost long ago, started to hammer against its prison. "You…you read about my father."

"You know I didn't, ma'am. You already got rid of every trace of him. You didn't want anyone to know what he did…what he did for *you*."

Tears battered her corneas, but she refused to let them escape. She narrowed her eyes in a desperate attempt to keep the salty water imprisoned.

"You have no idea what you're talking about..."

"You don't have children, Ms. Doubek," Vilém said. "I don't know if that was just your preference or if you were scared...scared, maybe, that you'd understand why he did it..."

"There is no excuse for what he did!" Alica screamed, stomping her foot, sending a tremble through the old building. "And if you're trying to say that his ghost is here, waiting for me to say I'm sorry, waiting for me to say I still love him, he's got another thing coming!"

Tears broke through her barrier, dripping down her face as she cried out. "You hear that, Father? I'm still angry! I will never stop being angry at you!"

Vilém shook his head, his teensy smile vanishing. "Ms. Doubek, your father was many things, but y'know...he was a good father. That may not make him a good person, but he put you above everything. Even himself. Your emotions are yours, and he doesn't want you to stop being angry at him. He wants you to stop being angry at yourself."

She wiped her tears away with her sleeve, seething at Vilém. "I am *not* angry at myself, I am *not*!"

"You blame yourself for what he did. You think because he sacrificed your friends for you, that guilt is yours. That's why you gave your rations to the other girls in the barrack..."

"Shut up..."

"That's why you've never let yourself smile or dance or have fun, not once in your whole life..."

"*Shut! Up!*" She charged at him, wielding her pointer like a sword. Vilém was ready. As she raised her little weapon to smack him, he dodged and grabbed her hand. She screeched.

"Let go of me!"

"Sure thing, ma'am," Vilém said, pulling the pointer out of her grasp and releasing her. He stepped back and, holding the pointer behind his back, offered her a hand.

"May I have a dance?" he asked, bowing towards her. She looked at him as though he had just suggested the world was flat.

"Excuse me?" she gasped.

"You don't deserve to be miserable all the time, Alica. What happened wasn't your father's fault, and it wasn't your fault. Blame the Nazis be mad at your father for what he did, but please stop being so angry all the time. You deserve to smile."

She covered her mouth with her hands, her eyes betraying her, shimmering with want as she looked down at his outstretched hand. Her foot committed treason by daring to tap.

"I can't..." she whispered. Vilém shrugged.

"Fine! Then I'll dance alone!" he declared. He twirled the pointer like it was a cane and began to dance just like she had when she was a child: with no sense of step and no skill whatsoever, with reckless joy.

"Rehor, stop, stop, you're in a barrack! People died here!" Alica shrieked, and he grinned when he heard suppressed amusement in her voice. She pressed her hands against her lips, desperately trying to keep her long-gone smile from returning.

"And you lived! Isn't that great?" Vilém cried.

"No, no it is not!" Alica insisted, sobs starting to wrack her old body. "I didn't deserve it!"

"You *all* deserved to live and laugh and dance! The Nazis took that from all of you! Take it back!"

"You're so..." she started to say, but before she could accuse him of being stupid or irreverent or horrible, he danced right into his laptop. He stepped on the machine, cracking the keyboard, and jumped back, falling to the floor with a yelp.

"So make life worthwhile...
Come on and smile, darn ya', smile!"

Despite the terrible damage done to the computer, the old song continued to play. Vilém, dazed, rolled over and looked towards his laptop, his face turning red when he saw what he had done. He looked up at Alica, grinned, and shrugged.

"Whoops!" he cried, and the dam broke. Alica's hands flew from her mouth to her sides. She didn't just smile, she laughed. It was the strangest, most beautiful noise he had ever heard: an extinct laugh returning from the grave. Hoarse and clumsy like a child singing. She laughed so hard that she fell to her knees, so hard that tears conquered her eyes.

"Oh, you're so stupid!" she howled. She laughed and cried and smiled, and her smile was even lovelier than it had been when she was a child. It was a smile that had been waiting a lifetime to come out, and it was worth the wait.

Vilém sighed happily and collapsed to the floor, shutting his eyes.

"Mission accomplished," he whispered, and he heard the Rabbi's cracking voice echo from faraway.

You're a miracle, Vilém. You are an amazing man, and you will be an amazing father. Good luck...and thank you.

And with that, the Rabbi's spirit disappeared, and the only spirit left in Barrack Two was someone else, someone Vilém could sense was seething.

"Well..." Vilém sneered at Kommandant Gerber's furious ghost as Alica Doubek's melodious laughter drove the wicked phantom from Barrack Two. "You lose."

And the Jewish woman's laughter was so raucous that Vilém barely heard the Nazi's parting remark.

Not yet.

ACKNOWLEDGMENTS

Thank you for reading Barrack Two!
The final book in the Barracks Series, *Barrack One*, will
be available on January 28th, 2021!
Elyse Hoffman's next full-length novel, *The Book of Uriel*,
is available for preorder today! A heartbreaking and
touching tale, a blend of Jewish folklore and historical
fiction that will fascinate fans of *The Barracks* and *The
Book Thief*, *The Book of Uriel* will be released on January
26th, 2021.
If you would like to read more stories like this one,
follow Project 613 on Twitter @Project613Books, on
Facebook, and sign up for updates at Project613Pub-
lishing.com!